Not So Rotten Ralph

Written by Jack Gantos

Illustrated by Nicole Rubel

Houghton Mifflin Company
Boston 1994

For Francis

J.G.

The character of Rotten Ralph was originally
created by Jack Gantos and Nicole Rubel.

Text copyright © 1994 by John B. Gantos, Jr.
Illustrations copyright © 1994 by Nicole Rubel

Library of Congress Cataloging-in-Publication Data

Gantos, Jack.
   Not so Rotten Ralph / by Jack Gantos ; illustrated by Nicole
Rubel.
      p.   cm.
      Summary: Sarah's mischievous cat, Rotten Ralph, is sent to feline
finishing school, but Sarah finds she liked him better the way he
was.
      ISBN 0-395-62302-2
      [1. Cats—Fiction.   2. Behavior—Fiction.]   I. Rubel, Nicole,
ill.   II. Title.
PZ7.G15334No   1994   93-759
[E]—dc20   CIP
                             AC

Printed in the United States of America

WOZ   10   9   8   7   6   5   4   3   2   1

One morning when Sarah came down for
breakfast, Rotten Ralph was making blueberry
pancakes. "Please don't make a mess," said Sarah.

But Ralph didn't listen. He sprayed whipped cream all over the kitchen.

"Just go outside and play," groaned Sarah.

Rotten Ralph hid inside the mailbox and
surprised the mailman. The mail flew all over.
"Stop that, Ralph," said Sarah. "When are you
going to learn to behave?"

When Sarah picked up the mail, she saw an ad for
Mr. Fred's Feline Finishing School.
"Ralph," said Sarah, "this is just what you need."

When they arrived at the school, Sarah said
goodbye to Ralph. "I want you to do exactly as
they say," she said.

Rotten Ralph wanted to go home.

But Mr. Fred dragged him inside.

Mr. Fred meant business. "These are the golden
rules and regulations," he instructed. "Follow
them and you'll learn how to be good."
"Not me," Ralph thought. "My rule is to be rotten."
He made paper airplanes out of the golden rules.

Next they entered the SELF-CONTROL room.

"Don't touch anything," bellowed Mr. Fred. "Keep your paws to yourself."

Rotten Ralph had no self-control. He wanted to touch everything.

"Get a grip on yourself," said Mr. Fred. "I want your owner to be proud of you."

"Every good cat should have perfect table manners," said Mr. Fred.

Rotten Ralph ate everyone's spaghetti and chewed with his mouth open. Then he burped loudly.

"And no burping!" growled Mr. Fred. And he ordered Ralph to say "please and thank you" one hundred times.

Afterward they went to the FLUFF AND BUFF room
for a bath.

All of Ralph's fleas jumped on Mr. Fred.

"From now on, your fur will be brushed and your
teeth and nails will shine," ordered Mr. Fred.

"This feels horrible," Ralph cried.

At last they went into the final finishing room.

Mr. Fred made certain that all the cats acted alike.

"Repeat after me," sang Mr. Fred. He held up a gold watch on a long chain and swung it back and forth. "I am a good cat."

"I am a good cat," Ralph mumbled to himself.

"I am a good cat . . . I am a good cat . . ."

That afternoon Sarah arrived for Ralph's graduation. He received his diploma for PERFECT FELINE BEHAVIOR.

"Oh, Ralph," sighed Sarah, "I'm so proud that you have changed your rotten ways."

"He'll never be rotten again," said Mr. Fred.

When they got home, Sarah awarded Ralph with
a celebration. All of Ralph's friends had a great
time. But Ralph just slept.

"What's wrong, Ralph?" cried Sarah. "You used to
be the life of the party."

After the guests left the party, Sarah
made funny faces at Ralph. She played with his cat
toys. But nothing made Ralph feel rotten. He just
purred like a good cat.
"Wake up!" shouted Sarah. "I want my old Ralph
back."

She chased a mouse. She climbed the curtains.
She even ate a goldfish.

She opened his eyes. She stood him up. She threw a bucket of ice water on his face. She lifted him onto the chandelier and gave him a push.

Ralph swung back and forth until he remembered how good it felt to be rotten. He stuck his tongue out at Sarah. He growled a rotten growl.

Then he dropped down onto Sarah's lap.

"I'm glad my Rotten Ralph is back," sighed Sarah.

She gave Ralph a big hug.

"Me too," thought Ralph as he ripped up his

diploma.